THIS WALKER BOOK BELONGS TO:

_____

_____

_____

_____

For Lon,
who loves those babies,
ducks, and me

A.H.

For my three heroines and a hero –
Amelia, Helen, Lucy and David

J.B.

First published 1996 by Walker Books Ltd
87 Vauxhall Walk, London SE11 5HJ

This edition produced 2000 for The Book People Ltd
Hall Wood Avenue, Haydock, St Helens WA11 9UL

2 4 6 8 10 9 7 5 3 1

Text © 1996 Amy Hest
Illustrations © 1996 Jill Barton

This book has been typeset in
Opti Lucius Ad Bold.

Printed in Hong Kong

British Library Cataloguing in Publication Data
A catalogue record for this book is
available from the British Library.

ISBN 0-7445-5220-6

Baby Duck
and the
New Eyeglasses

by **Amy Hest**

illustrated by **Jill Barton**

WALKER BOOKS
AND SUBSIDIARIES
LONDON · BOSTON · SYDNEY

B aby Duck was looking in the mirror.
She was trying on her new eyeglasses.
They were too big on her baby face.
They pushed against her baby cheeks.
And she did not look like Baby.

Baby came slowly down the stairs.
"Park time!" said Mr Duck. "Grandpa
will be waiting in his boat at the lake!"
"How sweet you look in your
new eyeglasses!" cooed Mrs Duck.
"Don't you love them?"

"No," Baby said.

"How well you must see in your
 new eyeglasses!" clucked Mr Duck.

"Don't you like them just a little?"

"No," Baby said.

The Duck family went out of the front door. Mr and Mrs Duck hopped along. "Hop down the lane, Baby!" Baby did not hop. Her glasses might fall off.

Mr and Mrs Duck danced along.

"Dance down the lane, Baby!"

Baby did not dance.

Her glasses might fall off.

When they got to the park, Baby sat in the grass behind a tree. She sang a little song.

"Poor, poor Baby, she looks ugly
In her bad eyeglasses.
Everyone can play but me,
Poor, poor, poor, poor Baby."

Grandpa came up the hill.

"Where's that Baby?" he called.

"I'm afraid she is hiding," Mrs Duck sighed.

"She does not like her new eyeglasses,"
worried Mr Duck.

Grandpa sat in the grass behind the tree.
"I like your hiding place," he whispered.
"Thank you," Baby said.

Grandpa peered round the
side of the tree.
"I see new eyeglasses," he
whispered. "Are they blue?"
"No," Baby said.

"Green?" Grandpa whispered.
"No," Baby said.

"Cocoa brown?"
Grandpa whispered.

Baby came out from behind the tree. Grandpa folded his arms. "Well," he said, "I think those eyeglasses are *very* fine."

"Why?" Baby asked.

"Because they are red like mine!" Grandpa said.

Grandpa kissed Baby's cheek. "Can you still run to the lake and splash about?"

Baby ran and splashed.

Then she
splashed harder.

Her glasses
did not fall off.

"Can you still twirl three times without falling down?"

Baby twirled.

One,

two,

three.

She did not fall down.
And her glasses did
not fall off.

"Come with me, Baby.
I have a surprise," Grandpa said.

They walked down to the pier.
Grandpa's boat was bobbing on the
water. There was another boat, too.
"Can you read what it says?"
Grandpa asked.
Baby read, "B-a-b-y."
The letters were very clear.

Then Grandpa and Mr and Mrs Duck
sat in Grandpa's boat. But Baby sat in
her boat and she sang a new song.

"I have nice new eyeglasses!
I look like my Grandpa.
My rowing-boat is lots of fun,
And I can read my name on it."

MORE WALKER PAPERBACKS
For You to Enjoy

Also by Amy Hest

IN THE RAIN WITH BABY DUCK
illustrated by Jill Barton

Baby Duck hates the rain. Mother and Father Duck can't understand it. But Grandpa can and he knows how to make Baby happy!

"Brilliant combination of text and pictures...
A night after night book for two to four-year-olds." *The Sunday Telegraph*

0-7445-6323-2   £4.99

ROSIE'S FISHING TRIP
illustrated by Paul Howard

"The harmony between the old and the very young has not often been shown as effectively as it is here...
Little girls will love this one." *The Junior Bookshelf*

0-7445-4703-2   £4.99

JAMAICA LOUISE JAMES
illustrated by Sheila White Samton

Jamaica Louise James lives in New York with her Mama and Grammy and she loves to draw and tell stories about the things she sees around her. This colourful story tells of her big, cool idea for brightening up Grammy's birthday.

0-7445-5293-1   £4.99